Minnie & Moo

and the SEVEN WONDERS OF THE WORLD

Minnie & Moo

and the SEVEN WONDERS OF THE WORLD

Written and illustrated by Denys Cazet

A Richard Jackson Book

Atheneum Books for Young Readers

New York   London   Toronto   Sydney   Singapore

Atheneum Books for Young Readers
An imprint of Simon & Schuster
Children's Publishing Division
1230 Avenue of the Americas
New York, New York 10020
Copyright © 2003 by Denys Cazet
A shorter version of this story appeared nationally in
newspapers as part of the Breakfast Serials™ Program.
Book design by Kristin Smith
The text of this book is set in Horley Old Style.
The illustrations are rendered in pencil.
Printed in the United States of America
First Edition
2 4 6 8 10 9 7 5 3 1
Library of Congress Cataloging-in-Publication Data
Cazet, Denys.
Minnie and Moo and the seven wonders of the world /
Denys Cazet.
p.   cm.
"A Richard Jackson book."
Summary: Two cows try to save their farm by creating
seven wonders and asking the other animals for
donations to see them, but there is a wondrous
and frightening creature in the woods that
could foil the plan.
ISBN 0-689-85330-0
[1. Cows—Fiction. 2. Domestic animals—
Fiction. 3. Rhinoceroses—Fiction. 4. Farm life—
Fiction. 5. Humorous stories.] I. Title.
PZ7.C2985 Men 2003
[Fic]—dc21   2002002195

Bill Civitello

for then and now

contents

Minnie & Moo

The Night Before

Minnie and Moo strolled to the top of their favorite hill. They leaned against the old oak tree and watched the summer day give way to the summer night.

A light came on in the farmhouse. They could see Mrs. Farmer setting the table and Mr. Farmer reading the newspaper in his favorite chair.

Minnie waved to Bea and Madge Holstein, their two best friends, as they hurried past on their way to the barn for the night. Moo didn't seem to notice. She watched the great stacks of thunderclouds drifting across the horizon. She watched the long shadows of the pines on Wilkersons' farm creeping up the far hill. Moo wondered about the clouds. She wondered about the shadows.

Minnie looked at Moo. "You're thinking again," she said.

Moo sat down. "How did you know?"

"It's in the air," said Minnie. "Everyone else is settling in for the night, and your brain is cooking on all four burners."

Moo sighed. She looked at the grass. She tugged at a tuft of poppies. "I have thoughts," she said softly.

"Moo," said Minnie, "it is much too late for thinking. You know what that extra thought does to you in the evenings."

Moo picked a dandelion. She held it up against the setting sun and turned it slowly.

"Thinking is not healthy," continued Minnie. "Thinking leads to sleepless nights, heartache, and torpid bowels."

Moo lay back on the cool grass. She

blew on the dandelion and watched the feathery seeds rise up and float away in the light wind.

"Don't you ever think?" Moo asked.

"Please!" said Minnie. "When I am hungry, I eat. When I am thirsty, I drink. I don't have to think about it!"

"But, Minnie . . ."

"Tut-tut!" said Minnie. "When you were sick last winter, I did not have to think about taking care of you. You are my friend. One friend takes care of another. What is there to think about? There is too much thinking going on in the world and not enough doing."

"*That* is a thought!" said Moo.

"Moo!" gasped Minnie. "How can you say such a thing? I am a cow. I am much too busy to think."

Moo   touched   Minnie's   shoulder.

"Minnie," she said, "I am a cow . . . and I think."

Minnie sighed. She looked off into the distance. The hills were black against the fading light. "Mother Nature is an odd duck," she muttered.

"Aha!" said Moo. "There's another one!"

"Another what?" asked Minnie.

"Another thought!"

"Never!" said Minnie. "I was saying what

I know. I do not know because I think. I know because I see. I see. I say. I do."

Moo stared at Minnie for a moment. She put her arms behind her back and paced back and forth. Suddenly she twirled and said, "The farmer thinks, and look at all the wonderful things he can do."

Minnie folded her arms. "He does not *do* because he can think," Minnie said. "He *do* because he has thumbs!"

"And a bigger brain."

"Moo, every Thursday the farmer goes to the town council meeting in high spirits. When he comes home at night, he's all twisty and bent out of shape. The farmer's eyes are puffy and Mrs. Farmer has to put an ice bag on his head. He frumps and grumps and tosses and turns all night thinking about who said what, why they said it, and what he should have said but didn't. In the morning he wakes up worse than when he went to bed. He's still grumpy. He's cross. He burns the toast. He forgets to pay his electric bill.

"Mr. and Mrs. Farmer quarrel. He makes mistakes. Don't you remember the morning he hooked us up to the milker in the middle of a lightning storm?"

Moo remembered. How could she forget?

Every cow on the farm had had to take sitz baths for a week.

"I'm telling you, Moo, a bigger brain is not all it's cracked up to be."

"But . . . Minnie . . ."

"Moo, brains are overrated!"

"Minnie! What could be more important than the brain?"

"The stomach!" said Minnie. "The stomach is much more important."

"The stomach?" Moo repeated.

"Of course," said Minnie. "What matters more? Eating or thinking?"

Moo began to pace again. "If I do not eat," she muttered, "I will die. If I am dead, I cannot think. When I do not think, I fidget. Therefore, I would rather fidget while I am alive than fidget while I am dead."

Moo shrugged. "Eating is better than thinking, I think."

Minnie threw up her arms. "There you have it," she said. "It is why cows have several stomachs and farmers have only one. Now let's have no more of this! It's settled. Thinking is not healthy and—"

"What about dogs?" Moo asked.

"What?"

"What about dogs?" Moo repeated.

Minnie sighed. "What about them?"

"Dogs think," said Moo. "Rosie, Mrs. Farmer's cocker spaniel, sits on the back porch and stares off into space for hours at a time."

"Rosie is not thinking," said Minnie. "She is waiting for a thought."

"Okay," said Moo. "Then how about Labradors? . . . They think."

"No," said Minnie. "Labradors do not think. They please."

"How about cats?" said Moo. "When

Rufus catches a mouse in the barn, he plans, he schemes, he thinks."

"No," said Minnie. "Rufus never has to think. He simply does. He knows where the mice live and lies in the sun enjoying a snooze. If a mouse comes by, he will catch it. If he is in a playful mood, he will tease the bejabbers out of it. If he happens to be hungry, he will eat it. None of that requires thinking."

"I'll bet the mouse is thinking," said Moo.

"He shouldn't!" said Minnie. "He should be doing what he needs to do and watch where he's doing it. Forget the thinking and do the doing."

Moo turned away from Minnie and looked out across the farm toward the distant hills and the setting sun. She sighed and then sat down next to Minnie. "I guess you are right," she said. "I don't know why I have thoughts. They just seem to show up without being invited."

Minnie smiled. "We are what we are," she said, patting Moo on the arm. "Some things never change."

"That's all right with me," said Moo.

"Me too," said Minnie.

Together they watched the last rays of the sun fade in the western sky.

"Yesterday," said Minnie, "the night sky was red. Tonight it is orange."

Moo put her arm around Minnie.

"I wonder why," she said.

Not-So-Good News

Moo huffed and puffed up the hill. When she reached the top, she stopped to catch her breath in the shade of the old oak tree.

"Minnie," she gasped, "I have some not-so-good news. I heard the farmer talking. I heard him say, 'sell the farm.' He was talking to Mrs. Farmer when he said it. What are we going to do?"

Minnie sat in a green lawn chair. She wore a terry-cloth robe. Her head was wrapped in a pink towel, and one hoof was soaking in a tub of hot water.

"Minnie, did you hear me?" asked Moo,

pacing nervously back and forth. "I don't think the farmer has any money. If he doesn't have any money, he will have to sell the farm!"

Minnie looked through a box of chocolates that was sitting on her lap. There were more empty chocolate wrappers than filled ones. "Moo, can't you see I'm busy?" she said. Minnie took her foot out of the water and pointed to a bump on her toe. "I have a grunion!"

Moo looked at the bump. "That's called a 'bunion,'" she said. "A grunion is a fish."

"Grunion, bunion," said Minnie. "I say grunion and you say bunion. I say potato and you say po-taw-toe. I say tomato and you say toe-ma-toe. What's the—"

"Minnie! Please listen."

"Moo, will you relax?" said Minnie. "The farmer is always talking about selling

the farm. He's always complaining about
something: the weather, the price of hay,
the mayor, taxes, his back, how they don't
make things like they used to, and so on
and so forth! He's just a grumpy old man.
Now sit down. Have a chocolate."

Minnie handed Moo the box of candy.
Moo looked at the empty wrappers. She
looked at the few chocolates that were left.

They had all been squeezed. "Minnie, all these chocolates have been—"

Minnie sighed. "I was looking for a cream," she said. "Those are semisweet caramel. I don't mind semisweet caramel. But I prefer—"

"Minnie, please. This is serious," said Moo. "I heard the words 'sell the farm'!" Moo began pacing again. "I've got to think of something," she muttered.

"Oh, no, you don't!" said Minnie. "We are cows. Everyone knows what happens when you start thinking, Moo. Believe me, I know. Remember the trip to the moon on the farmer's tractor?"

Moo shrugged.

"Remember your idea about dressing up and going to the farmer's birthday party? We almost ended up as hamburger patties on his barbecue!"

"I know," said Moo. "But—"

"And the trip to Paris," Minnie continued. "You said France must be close because you saw Mrs. Farmer come home with a loaf of French bread."

"I know," said Moo. "But this is different. This is—"

"Moo," Minnie said gently, "look around you. The grass is growing, soft and green. The fish in the stream are enjoying life under the shade of the willow tree. The sky is clear and blue. The wind is carrying flower seeds all over the world, and the sun is warming the faces of the new kittens behind the barn. All of these wonderful things are happening without thinking. They are just doing."

"But, Minnie," protested Moo, "I—"

"Tut-tut," Minnie interrupted. "I'm not finished. I talked to you last night about this very thing. The farmer thinks. Where does it get him? He goes to town council meetings and argues with the mayor. He comes home and thinks about what he said and what he should have said. He can't sleep. In the morning he is even grumpier than usual. And why? Because of thinking!"

Moo sat down in the other lawn chair. She looked at Minnie and sighed. "Minnie," she said, putting her arm around her best friend, "you're right."

"I know," said Minnie, searching for another chocolate.

"But," said Moo, sitting back in her chair, "things will certainly be different around here after the farm is sold. Everything will change with new farmers."

Minnie picked up the last chocolate caramel and held it up to the sunlight.

Then she turned and looked at Moo. "What do you mean?"

Moo pointed at the empty box on Minnie's lap. "No more chocolate creams," she said. "No more chocolate, period! It will be back to hay three times a day, like the rest of the farms in the world."

Minnie stared at Moo. "You mean, no more cream puffs?" she said.

Moo shook her head. "No more," she said sadly.

Minnie frowned. "What about my espresso machine?"

"Gone," said Moo.

"Hot tub?"

"Gone," repeated Moo.

"Electric hair dryer?"

"Gone."

"My lipsticks? My skin creams? My bath

oils? My favorite red dress with the silver sequins and plunging neckline?"

"Gone, gone, gone," said Moo.

Minnie grabbed Moo. "*Moo!* We've got to *do* something!" she cried. "I don't want to live like an animal!"

Moo stood up and looked at Minnie. "If only we could find a way to earn some money. Some way to help the farmer, some way to save the farm. If we . . ." Moo stopped speaking. She bent over and looked closely at the lump on Minnie's foot. "Wait a minute," she mumbled. "What's this?"

"My grunion?" said Minnie.

"Bunion," Moo said. "Minnie, do you see what I see?"

Minnie looked at the bump on her foot.

"All I see is a sore . . . wait a minute. I *do* see something. I see a face!"

"Yes!" cried Moo. "And not just any face. That is the face that is going to save our farm!"

"Who is it?" Minnie asked.

"George Washington!" said Moo.

The Plan

Minnie looked at her bunion. "I don't get it," she said. "How is George Washington's face on a bunion going to save the farm?"

"Minnie, don't you see?" said Moo. "Everyone loves an oddity. Everyone loves a mystery. They may say they don't, but sooner or later curiosity gets the better of them. There isn't an animal on this farm who wouldn't pay to see a bunion with the face of the father of our country on it."

Moo pointed to Minnie's bump. *"That,"* she said, "is a presidential bunion!"

"Really?" said Minnie.

"Really," said Moo, pacing back and forth again. "But George will be free of

charge. We need to convince everyone that what we say is true. That way, they'll believe the other things as well."

"Other things?" said Minnie.

"Of course," said Moo. "The other mysteries on the farm. Life's puzzles, the unexplained, the wonders of the world.

That's it! *See the Seven Wonders of the World!*"

Minnie stood up and looked across the farm. "Moo, I don't see any wonders," she said. "I see a farmhouse, a barn, and some chickens."

"But I do," said Moo. "I see the Presidential Bunion. I see the Bermuda Triangle. I see the Mystery Spot, UFOs, FLUs!"

"FLUs?" said Minnie. "What's a FLU?"

"You know," said Moo, pointing toward the sky. "FLU. F-L-U. Flying Long Underwear."

Minnie looked up into the sky. She looked at Moo and sighed. "That's only five wonders," she said.

Moo closed her eyes and pointed into the distance. "I see the Rock That Never Moves," she said.

"That's six!" said Minnie.

"And Big Hoof!" Moo yelled.

"Big Hoof?" said Minnie. "Who's Big Hoof?"

"You've never heard of Big Hoof?"

Minnie shook her head.

"They say Big Hoof is the missing link between dinosaurs and cows. Some animals claim to have seen her in Wilkerson's Woods. Her footprints are huge."

Minnie looked toward the dark woods at the edge of the farm. "Really?" she said.

"Well, I've never seen her," said Moo. "But listen, Minnie. No one will believe your bunion has the face of George Washington on it. But once they see it, they will believe it. After that they'll believe anything!"

Minnie shook her head. "You make me nervous," she said. "Every time you get an idea, it starts up one way and ends up another."

"Minnie," said Moo softly, "I'm just trying to save the farm."

"I know," said Minnie. "But it sounds like . . . like . . . cheating."

"No, no," said Moo. "It's being creative. It's more like taking something old and making something new out of it. Like making up your own recipe."

Minnie let out a tired breath of air. She looked at Moo. "Making up your own recipe?" she said.

"Yes," said Moo. "All you have to do is take a little something that's sort of true and mix it with something that's sort of not true. Then you toss it around a little and sauce it up a bit. Soon you have something new, different, more interesting, and more tasty."

"Sounds like a salad," said Minnie.

"No," said Moo thoughtfully. "More

27

like a bowl of mock turtle soup. There really isn't any turtle in mock turtle soup, but it's still a bowl of soup."

"More like a bowl of fibs," said Minnie. "I don't like it!"

Minnie looked out over the farm. She saw her friends Bea and Madge Holstein standing near the chicken coop talking to some mutual friends. She saw the farmer going into the barn next to his tractor and Mrs. Farmer carrying out the wash. Minnie remembered all the wonderful years everyone at the farm had spent together.

Moo sighed.

"Minnie," she said, "what will happen to all the animals on the farm if we don't do something?"

"We?" Minnie said. "How does it always end up with 'we'? Your ideas are like an invisible net. You cast it out as 'I' and it comes back loaded with 'we.'"

Moo smiled at Minnie.

"Okay, okay!" Minnie said. "I hope I'm not going to regret this. What do you want me to do first?"

"Make posters!" said Moo, sitting down. She put a box of felt pens and some paper on the table.

Then she wrote in large letters:

SAVE OUR FARM!

and for a $mall donation...

See The Seven Wonders of The World!

★ The PRESIDENTIAL BUNION ★

• The rock that NEVER moves! •

★ The MILLION-year-old landing site of a U.F.O. ★
(and the hubcap it left behind)

★ The BERMUDA TRIANGLE ★
(Walk through Boohoo Land and hear the WELL of TROUBLES speak!)

• The MYSTERY SPOT •
Watch your legs grow longer on one side and shrink on the other!

★ The F.L.U. MYSTERY   ★ BIG HOOF
Why does FLYING LONG UNDERWEAR   Is she watching?
flock together on Thursdays?

★ Thursday !! TOMORROW 9:00am !!
UNDER THE OLD OAK TREE

SEE THE WORLD'S MOST ASTOUNDING MYSTERY!
★ FREE ! at NO COST to you ! (donations welcome)

"There!" said Moo. "That's what the posters should look like. You can help by making more. When you're done, just tack them up around the farm."

Minnie read the poster. "Moo," she said, "I know where the Presidential Bunion is, but where are all these other 'wonders'?"

Moo stood up. "Out there," she said, sweeping her arm in the air. "Out there." Then she turned and started to walk away.

"Moo, where are you going?" asked Minnie.

Moo winked. "I'm going to cook up some new recipes," she said. "You know, take a little of the truth and mix it in with a little of the not so true."

"Mock turtle soup," said Minnie.

"Right," said Moo.

Minnie pointed toward Wilkerson's

Woods. "Moo, don't forget there are some things that should be left alone."

"Minnie, tomorrow the Seven Wonders tour will start here with the Presidential Bunion. Then, one by one, we'll find the other mysteries along the road. Some will be in the meadow and in the farmer's garden, and some will be at the edge of Wilkerson's Woods.

A cool breeze blew across the hill, and Minnie shivered. "That's what I mean," she said. "The woods are dark. Things live in there. Maybe things you think you made up, but didn't. Maybe there really is a—a . . ."

Moo looked out toward Wilkerson's Woods. "You mean—"

"Big Hoof!" Minnie whispered.

The Presidential Bunion

The next morning a light, cool breeze blew across the farm. A few low clouds drifted far away in the blue of the dawn sky.

The animals gathered under the old oak tree at the top of the hill. They milled around and chatted about the posters. They talked to Moo as she passed out warm cocoa in paper cups.

Moo was dressed in a tuxedo with tails. She wore a top hat that had 1939 WORLD'S FAIR printed on it. Minnie sat at a table. She wore a purple bathrobe with gold trim. A turban with a red plastic jewel in the center sat tightly on her head. Her foot rested on a plump feather pillow. The Presidential Bunion was covered by an argyle sock.

A bowling ball sat on the table on a square of velvet. Next to the bowling ball was a large jar with a label that read: DONATIONS WELCOME. A sign on the table read:

Madame Minnie
Mistress of the Presidential Bunion
Teller of Fortunes

Moo waved everybody over to Madame Minnie's table. The animals crowded together to try to get a better view of the Presidential Bunion.

"We are gathered here today," said Moo, "to see the Seven Wonders of the World and, most important of all, to save our—"

"Never mind that stuff!" shouted Elvis, the rooster. "Let's see the grunion!"

"Bunion!" snapped Madame Minnie. "A grunion is a fish!"

"Yeah, yeah," said Elvis. "I'm not putting a nickel in that jar until I see it!"

"You can wait your turn," said Madame

Minnie. "Bea and Madge are going to be first!"

Moo removed the argyle sock with a flourish. "Tra la!" she shouted.

Bea and Madge looked at the lump. They looked closer. "Minnie," Madge whispered, "I don't see any president."

Minnie looked. The swelling had gone

down during the night. "Uh-oh," she said. "Moo?"

"Oops," said Moo, looking at the bunion. She glanced over at Bea. "The mystery of the bunion." She nodded solemnly. "Yes. The mystery of the bunion. What magic lies within? What other presidential faces might appear to those with the vision to see Mother Nature's magic?"

Bea stared at the bunion.

"Bea Holstein is now looking," Moo announced, "and she sees the face of . . ."

Bea stared at the bump.

"She sees the face of a president . . ."

Bea looked at Moo. Moo raised her arms and yelled, "*She sees the face of President Abraham*—"

"*Lincoln!*" shouted Bea.

"*Alleluia!*" cried Moo.

Bea threw her arms around Madge. "I saw Mother Nature's magic," she sobbed out.

"May I look?" one of the sheep asked meekly. He stared at the bump. "Ohhh," he moaned. "It is the face of 'he with the electric clippers.' The one who clips our wool and makes us naked!" The sheep blushed. The flock gave him a group hug.

"Let's hear it for the sheep!" Moo shouted. Everyone applauded.

A small pig named Hamlet looked at the bump. "Oh, my," he said. "I see the face of Mr. Bartolucci, the butcher."

"*Aggggggggggggg!*" cried the other pigs.

"Three cheers for the pigs!" shouted Moo.

"Fake!" cried Elvis. He folded his wings. "Magic, schmagic. I don't see any grunion!"

Minnie glared at the rooster. "Bunion!" she said.

Moo whispered in Minnie's ear. Minnie nodded. "There is a reason," said Moo, pointing at the rooster, "that you haven't seen a face on the magic bunion."

"Oh, yeah?" said Elvis. "And what's that?"

"Because you haven't looked!" said Moo. "But before you do, Madame Minnie will gaze into her crystal ball and tell you what you will see!"

Elvis shrugged. "No skin off my beak!" he said.

"Ooohhhh," Minnie moaned. Her eyes were closed as she rubbed the top of the bowling ball. "Ooohhhhhhhh!"

"Leg cramps?" Madge asked.

Minnie stopped moaning. "What do you mean, 'leg cramps'?"

"You sound just like Elsie Holstein did when she got leg cramps from jogging," said Madge. "Remember, Bea? She was hopping around like a twelve-hundred-pound toad and—"

"That wasn't the worst part," interrupted Bea. "She—"

"I'm not having leg cramps," Minnie said crossly. "I'm having vibrations. A kind of vision!" Minnie glared at Madge. "Are you calling me a toad?"

"No," said Madge. "I said Elsie was hopping around like a—"

"See these?" Minnie interrupted, pulling up her robe. "Do these look like a pair of legs that belong on a frog?"

"Toad," said Bea.

"Toad, frog . . . what's the difference?" said Minnie irritably. "I know cows who would give their left horn for a pair of legs like these!"

"Frogs don't have warts," said Bea.

"What?" said Minnie.

"Warts," said Madge. "Toads have warts, but frogs—"

"Oh, I see," said Minnie. "Now you're saying my legs have warts!"

"No," said Bea. "She meant—"

"I know what she meant," Minnie snapped. She pointed at her toe. "That," she said, "is a grunion. Not a wart! A presidential grunion!"

"Bunion," said Elvis. "A grunion is a fish."

Minnie glared at Elvis.

"Madame Minnie, please," said Moo. "Calm down. You have great legs. Time to move on. We have other fish to fry."

"Grunion?" Elvis said.

"Please!" said Moo.

Madame Minnie took a deep breath. "Where was I?" she said.

"You were in the middle of a vision," said Moo.

Madame Minnie cleared her throat and then began to moan. "Ooohhhhhhhhh."

Moo lay her arm across her forehead. She closed her eyes. "What face does Madame Minnie see?" she asked.

"I see the face of someone so beautiful, he makes the sun rise," said Madame Minnie. "Someone who is handsome, noble, brave, intelligent, modest—"

"That's me!" shouted Elvis.

"*Alleluia!*" Moo cried out. "Elvis has seen the wonder of Mother Nature's magic!"

The animals cheered.

Minnie passed around the donation jar.

Moo smiled at Elvis. "You're so lucky," she said. "You have the eyes of an eagle. What a wonderful gift."

"Gift?" said Elvis. "What gift? Was I supposed to get a gift? Where is it? Is it too big to carry? Do we need the tractor? A crane? Okay, forget the crane. We can all help carry it back to the farm. Friends help one another. Right?"

"On to the second mystery!" declared Minnie.

Elvis looked around. "Wait!" he cried. "My gift. Oh! I get it. It's small. That's okay. Sometimes big things come in small packages. Like jewels. Rubies are small. I think an emerald would go better with my eyes. I like green. Money is green."

"On to the Rock That Never Moves!" Moo shouted.

"What about my gift?" asked Elvis.

Everyone followed Minnie and Moo over the hill and down to the road. The sun was high in the sky, and the clouds had moved on toward the east. A light wind hurried past as Moo suddenly stopped. She looked up and down the road.

"What?" said Minnie.

"The Rock That Never Moves!" said Moo.

"What about it?" asked Minnie.

"It's gone!" said Moo.

Motherhood and a Hubcap

The animals formed a circle around a large hole in the middle of the road. "The rock was here yesterday," said Moo.

"Well," said Hamlet, "it's gone today!"

"Just like my gift," Elvis muttered.

"Moo," said Madge, "are you sure this is the right spot?"

"Hmm," said Moo. "If that rock moved, it must have had a very good reason to do so!"

Bea looked into the hole.

"I see little rocks," she said. "Pebbles."

"That's it!" said Moo.

"What's it?" Madge asked.

"That's the reason the Rock That Never

Moves moved," Moo declared. "Those aren't pebbles. Those are baby rocks!"

"So that's where rocks come from," said Bea.

"I always wondered," said Madge.

"That rock was a mother rock," Moo announced. "She'd been sitting in this hole for a squillion years, having those pebbles."

"I know what that's like," said one of the sheep. "I had triplets once."

"Triplets," said a pig. "That's nothing. I had fifteen piglets last spring. Talk about taking a squillion years!"

"Did I ever tell you about the time I had twins in the middle of my morning milking?" asked Bea.

"Only about a billion times," said Madge.

"You think *that's* something," said an

older mother from somewhere in the crowd. "Listen to *this*. . . ."

Soon all the mothers began discussing how long it had taken to have their children and how grateful they were not to be elephants or mother rocks.

"Whoa, whoa," said Elvis, looking into the hole. "You're trying to tell me those are baby rocks? You want me to put a nickel in the donation jar just because you say those are baby rocks? A whole nickel?"

Moo reached into the hole. She took out the smallest pebble and held it gently in her hoof. "Hello, little pebble," she said.

Madge touched the pebble. "She must've just had them," she said. "This one's still warm."

"Isn't it cute?" said Moo.

"Yeah, cute," said Elvis, picking up

another pebble. He rocked the pebble
back and forth and sang:

> *"Rock a bye, pebble,*
> *In the middle of the road,*
> *Along came a steamroller*
> *Sand à la mode!"*

All of the animals stared at him.

"That's not funny," said Bea.

"Put it back," said Minnie. "Mama
might show up any minute."

"Right," said Elvis. "Where is she?
Getting a snack at the gravel pit?"

Moo put the pebble she was holding
back in the hole. "It's not Mama you have
to worry about," she said.

Elvis rolled his eyes. "Really?" he said.

"Really," said Moo. She pointed to a
massive boulder that teetered at the edge

of an outcropping. "Do you see that big boulder?"

Elvis stared at the boulder above him. "What about it?"

Moo shrugged. "That's Daddy!"

"Whoa," said Elvis, putting the pebble gently back in the hole. "Just kidding," he said cheerfully.

Moo leaned closer to Minnie. "Moan," she whispered.

"Ooohhhhh!" moaned Madame Minnie. "Ooohhhhhh!"

"Madame Minnie is getting vibrations again!" Moo announced. "We must be approaching the Third Wonder of the World, the landing site of a UFO and the hubcap it left behind!"

"Where?" Minnie asked softly.

"To the left," whispered Moo. "At the edge of Wilkerson's Woods."

"Ooooohhhhhh!" moaned Madame Minnie again, waving her arms in the air. "I'm having a vision. I'm having a vision of—of . . ." Minnie opened one eye and looked at Moo.

"*That!*" shouted Moo, pointing to the ground. "We are standing in the middle of the ancient landing site of an alien spaceship. Thirty-seven years ago a UFO landed here and stole five pounds of fava beans and a half pound of okra from the farmer's field."

The animals looked at the grass that had been burned away in a large circle.

"*Yikes!*" they cried.

The sheep stepped out of the circle and looked around nervously.

Moo whispered to Minnie, "This is where the farmer had his summer burn pile. He burned it last week."

Minnie nodded.

The sheep looked up into the sky. "What if they come back shopping for another five pounds of fava beans and a half pound of okra?" asked one of them.

"Or even a quarter pound," added another.

"Or lamb chops," said Elvis.

"Ohhh," the sheep moaned.

"They could be here right now," said a sheep. "Watching. Waiting to do the alien pounce!"

A pinecone fell from a nearby tree and bounced in front of them. "Alien!" some-one shouted.

"They're back!" the sheep cried.

Minnie picked up the pinecone and held it in front of the sheep. "This," she said, "is a pinecone."

"How do you know?" asked a sheep.

Moo took the pinecone from Minnie. She looked it over carefully. "Hmm," she muttered. "How do we know?"

Minnie rolled her eyes. "How?" she said, pointing to the scraggy pine tree hanging over them. "That's how!"

Everyone looked up at the pine tree.

"Ohhh," gasped the sheep. "Look. The tree is full of them."

"Just like in my favorite movie," said Bea. *"Invasion of the Alien Fava Beans."*

"Ohhh!" moaned the sheep.

Madge stared at her sister. "Bea, what are you talking about."

"Don't you remember? In the movie the alien fava beans disguise themselves as ordinary pinecones so they can walk down the street without attracting attention. Then, when people aren't looking, the aliens slip up behind an okra and suck the blood out."

Madge looked at Minnie and sighed. "Bea, okra is a vegetable. It doesn't have any blood."

"Oh," said Bea. "Maybe it was a beet."

"Geez," said Elvis. "And they say chickens have small brains."

Moo pointed to a garbage-can lid that was leaning against a tree. "And *there*," she cried, "is the hubcap they left behind!"

Elvis walked over to the lid. He kicked it, and it rolled to the ground. "This looks like a garbage-can lid," said Elvis.

"If that's a garbage-can lid," said Moo, "where's the garbage can?"

Elvis shrugged. "How would I know?

Maybe it's in its nest having wastebaskets."

"Very funny," said Minnie. "If Moo says that's a hubcap from a spaceship, then that's what it is. Haven't you ever heard of mock turtle soup?"

Elvis stared at Minnie. "What?"

"I said—"

"Look at the size of that," said Madge. "It's huge."

"Of course," said Moo. "Alien hubcaps are always huge."

"Not that," said Madge. *"That!"*

Madge pointed to the ground near the edge of the woods.

"It's a giant footprint!" said Bea.

"There's more!" said Madge. "They lead into the woods."

Everyone was quiet. Their eyes followed the footprints that disappeared into the deep darkness of Wilkerson's Woods.

They listened to the wind moving through the trees.

Minnie winked at Moo. "Good job, Moo," she whispered. "Those look like real footprints."

"Minnie," said Moo softly.

"Oooohhhhhh," Minnie suddenly moaned. "I'm getting vibrations! I feel a vision coming on. I see, I see—"

"Minnie," said Moo again.

"Ooohhhhh!" continued Minnie.

"Minnie!"

"What?"

"I didn't make those footprints!"

The Well of Troubles

Minnie looked at the footprints.

They seemed to have been made by something very big and very heavy. "Moo," she whispered, "if you didn't make these footprints, then who did?"

Moo shook her head. "I don't know. I hope we haven't bitten off more than we can chew."

"Ohhh," Minnie groaned. "There's that 'we' again! Ooohhhh. Maybe it *is* Big Hoof! Ooohhhhh!"

Bea felt Minnie's forehead. "No vibrations," she said. "Are you having another vision, or are you getting leg—"

"Don't even say it!" said Minnie. "If you want to know what I see, I'll tell you. I see trouble!"

"Trouble?" said Madge. "What kind of trouble?"

"Big trouble," said Minnie. "Big trouble with big feet."

Moo raised her arms over her head. "Madame Minnie is having another vision!" she cried. "Pay attention, everybody!"

"Again?" said Minnie.

Moo nodded. "Please."

"Ooohhhhhhhh!" moaned Madame Minnie. "I'm having another vision. I see—"

"*Troubles!*" shouted Moo. "Madame Minnie sees the Well of Troubles in the Bermuda Triangle."

Madame Minnie closed her eyes. "Ooohhhhhhhh!" she moaned. "I see the

Well of Troubles in the Bermuda Triangle.
I see the strange and wonderful. And, for
a small donation, so will all of you."

Minnie swayed from side to side and
pointed toward the farmer's garden. Moo
held out the donation jar. Most of the
animals put money in it. When Elvis
thought no one was looking,
he took out fifteen cents.

The animals looked anxiously at the
gate . . . the gate that would lead them
into the secrets of the Fourth Wonder of
the World.

"And now," Moo cried out, "let us pass

through the portal of the Fourth Wonder of the World: the Bermuda Triangle. Let us stroll through Boohoo Land and gaze into the Well of Troubles. Let the mysteries of Mother Nature speak!"

The animals crowded through the gate. They stomped through the farmer's onion patch. The smell of crushed onions began to drift across the garden like an odorous ground fog.

Minnie fanned herself. Tears rolled down her cheeks. "I can see why you call it 'Boohoo Land,'" she said.

Moo dabbed her eyes. "I didn't think it would be this bad," she said.

The other animals wiped their eyes and peered into the dark, damp well at the edge of the onion patch. Something moved in the murky water.

"Nauuuughty," croaked a frog.

"Did you hear that?" said Bea.

"Nauuuughty," croaked the frog.

"I think it's talking to you," said Madge.

"Nauuuughty," croaked the frog.

"The well is speaking!" said one of the sheep. "Did you hear that?"

"Nauuuughty, nauuuughty," croaked the frog.

"I heard it!" said the smallest sheep.

"Nauuuughty, nauuuughty, nauuuughty," croaked the frog again.

The smell of the crushed onions grew stronger. Hamlet sniffed. "What?"

"The Well of Troubles has spoken!" cried the sheep. "It said we were naughty! Boohoo, we've been baaaaad. Real baaaaaaddd. Boohoo, boohoo."

The sheep milled about, kicking the grass and weeping.

Moo felt sorry for them. She wandered

over to the well. "You're not bad," she said. "Sometimes things happen. You stray from the flock. You get burrs in your wool. That doesn't make you—"

"Nauuughty," cried the sheep.

"No," said Moo, shaking her head. "What I'm trying to tell you is that sometimes it's difficult not to step in life's mud puddles—"

"*It was me!*" shouted Hamlet's uncle,

Snort. "I did it! I'm the one who jumped into the mud puddle! I sat in it all day and didn't share. I'm so sorry," he said with a sob.

Mort, another uncle of Hamlet's, stared sadly. "I'm sorry," he said, wiping away a tear. "I'm sorry I don't have anything to be sorry about."

"I don't know my times tables!" said Hamlet.

Moo looked at Minnie and shrugged.

The farmer's black Lab threw a paw around Rufus, the cat. Rufus was sniffling to himself at the edge of the garden. "I apologize," said the dog. "I'm sorry I chased you up the apple tree and made you stay there during the hailstorm."

Rufus dabbed his whiskers with his tail. "I should never have put that hair ball in your water bowl," he said.

Bea hugged Madge. "I'm sorry I scared you with the rubber spider and curdled your milk," said Bea.

"It's okay," said Madge. "I'm sorry about putting the bubble gum in your tuba."

"Hey!" said Elvis. "I'm sorry too. Okay? It wasn't my fault! The roosters at the Wilkersons' farm were having a birthday party for Little Willie. It was their fault for inviting me. They knew I was supposed to be with you in the coop sorting eggs. But, oh, no, they had to invite me to the party. I begged them not to invite me. 'Don't invite me,' I said. 'I want to be with my favorite chickens sorting eggs.' They made me go. They made me have fun. They made me put on the lampshade and wear it like a dress. They made me dance the hootchy-kootchy—"

He reached out toward the chickens. They watched him suspiciously for a moment and then began cackling to one another.

Minnie walked over to Moo. "This is too much, Moo," she said, blowing her nose. "My eyes are getting red."

Moo wiped the tears from her cheeks. "You're right," she said. "These onions are too strong. It's time to move on."

Suddenly, the chickens rushed into the

field and began pecking at Elvis. They chased him out the gate.

"It wasn't my fault!" Elvis shouted. "What do you expect? Ouch! I'm a rooster! Ouch! Ouch!" The chickens pecked and clucked. They chased Elvis down the road and into Wilkerson's Woods.

Minnie wiped a tear from her cheek. "Those are some onions!" she cried.

"Bermuda onions," said Moo. "The Bermuda Triangle. What other mysteries does Mother Nature have in store for us? Why does—"

"Look!" cried Minnie. "The chickens are coming back. They look scared. And there's Elvis. He's running right behind them!"

"Monster!" screamed Elvis. "Run for your lives!"

The Mystery Spot

The chickens jumped up and down and pointed toward the woods.

"Monster!" shouted Elvis again. He ran into the middle of the flock of chickens and fell on the ground. "It was huge," he gasped.

The sheep backed up the hill and huddled together behind a big tree.

"What happened to your feathers?" Madge asked.

"What?" wheezed Elvis.

"Your feathers," said Bea. "They're gone."

Elvis looked at himself. "Geez," he said. "I must have molted when I bolted!"

"So . . . what happened?" asked Hamlet.

"There I was," said Elvis, "alone, trying to protect my loved ones." Elvis blew a kiss to the chickens. "Then it jumped me from behind. It was huge. It had more horns than a herd of cattle. I pulled out my sword—"

"What sword?" said Minnie. "You didn't have a sword."

"How do you know?" said Elvis. "You weren't there!"

"Because you—"

"Elvis," said Moo calmly, "just tell us what happened."

Minnie leaned down and stared into Elvis's face. "The truth!" she said.

Elvis took a deep breath. "Okay," he said. "Okay. There we were. The chickens were pecking me on the noggin while I was calmly trying to explain the situation.

I know I should have been back at the coop sorting eggs. But it was Little Willie's birthday party. You can't just walk out on a party for Little Willie. Besides, I was having fun. Can't a rooster have a little fun? It wasn't my fault my rooster pal Pollo paid me thirty-five cents to kiss his sister. Thirty-five cents! I didn't really want to stay. But then someone says, 'I dare you,' and then it's 'I double dare you,' and then, before you know it, you're putting on a lampshade and doing the hootchy-kootchy and—"

"*Elvis!*" shouted Minnie. "What did you see in the woods?"

Everyone jumped.

"Geez!" said Elvis. "I was getting to that."

"Was it Big Hoof?" asked Bea.

"It was big everything. Big feet, big nose, and a butt bigger than a cow's. I know it's hard to imagine anything that big, but . . . I saw it!"

The four cows glared at Elvis.

"What?" said Elvis.

"Did it say anything?" Hamlet asked.

"It said, 'Foop,'" said Elvis.

"'Foop?'" repeated Moo.

"Foop," said Elvis.

"Just plain 'foop'?" said Moo.

"Foop!" said Elvis. "How many times do I have to say it? Foop, poop, soup, who cares? We're out of here! Come on, girls!" Elvis and a few of the chickens walked away.

Gradually, the sheep and a few of the pigs started to wander away as well.

Madge put her arm around Moo. "Moo," she said, "I know you and Minnie were just trying to save our farm. But maybe you should forget about it. Some things you can't change. Some things are too dangerous. Some things—"

"Forget about it?" said Moo. "You're saying give up? Just because Elvis saw— saw . . . something?"

"What about the chickens?" said Bea. "They saw something too."

Moo sighed. She sat down on a fallen tree. "I don't know what they saw," she muttered. "I thought I was doing the right

thing by making up the Seven Wonders. I thought we could have fun and save the farm at the same time." Moo looked at her friends. "I'm sorry," she said sadly.

Minnie sat down next to Moo. "Maybe there really is a Big Hoof," she said. "Doesn't that scare you?"

Moo nodded. "Yes, but not as much as losing our farm."

The rest of the animals sat down on the log. They sat quietly for a long time.

"Moo's right!" said Minnie suddenly. "We can't give up now. Maybe there's a Big Hoof and maybe there isn't. We have to help the farmer. It's our farm too!"

"But how do we get everyone to come back?" Bea asked.

Minnie reached into her robe and took out a Hershey's bar with almonds. "That's a good question," she said. When she finished the first candy bar, she took out a Snickers bar.

Madge and Bea stared at Minnie.

"What?"

"What else is in there?" Moo asked.

Minnie looked toward the distant hills. "Where?" she said.

"You know where," said Moo. "Open it up. I have an idea."

Minnie opened up her robe. Inside the lining there were six big pockets stuffed with snacks. "There," she said. "Now is everybody happy?"

"Wow," said Bea. "It looks like the inside of a vending machine. Candy bars on one side and soft drinks on the other!"

"A girl has to eat!" said Minnie. "You can't do all this exercise without fuel. Besides, energy bars are good for you."

Moo put her arm around Minnie.

"Minnie, I have an idea how we can get the others to come back."

Minnie glanced down the road and then back at Moo. She looked at the inside of her robe and the candy bars. "Oh!" she muttered and closed her robe tightly. "That's a very bad idea!"

"Minnie," said Moo softly, "you've got to share."

"Why?" said Minnie desperately.

"To save the farm," said Madge.

Moo touched Minnie's face. "Minnie," she said, "ask not what your farm can do for you, but what you can do for your farm."

Minnie sighed. "Okay," she said sadly.

Moo hugged Minnie. "Thank you."

"Can I keep the 3 Musketeers bar for myself?" Minnie asked. "It's my favorite."

"Of course," said Moo.

Minnie smiled weakly.

Moo walked out to the road. "Free snacks!" she shouted. "Free snacks for the friends of the Seven Wonders of the World. Come share the wealth of Mother Nature."

The animals stopped. They turned and looked back along the road at Moo.

Minnie walked over and stood next to her. "Let me try," she said. *"Free candy bars and soft drinks!"* she yelled. *"Come and get it!"*

The animals ran back toward Moo. They stopped in a cloud of dry dust that drifted across the road.

"Snacks?" said Elvis. "Where? Is this another cow trick like my disappearing gift?"

Minnie opened up her coat.

"Whoa!" said Elvis.

While they were all sitting under the oak tree eating and chatting, Elvis leaned over and whispered to Moo.

"Wisten," he said.

"What?" said Moo.

Elvis spit out a peanut. "Listen," he said. "I know what you cows are up to! You cows are going to take the money and go on a cruise to one of those islands like Huba. That's okay with me as long as I get my gift. Understand? I prefer cash! Speaking of cash, and just to show you my heart is in the right place, here's fifteen cents to help save the farm." Elvis winked, dropped the fifteen cents into the donation jar, and then strutted off.

"What was that all about?" Minnie asked.

"Who knows?" said Moo. "Why don't you have another vision while I clean up."

Minnie took a deep breath. "Ooohhhhh," moaned Madame Minnie.

The animals stood up and stretched. Moo walked up the hill.

"On to the Fifth Wonder," Minnie moaned. "The Mystery Spot!"

Madge passed the donation jar down the long line of animals as they marched single file along the side of the steep hill.

Moo stopped. "Here it is!" she cried. "The Fifth Wonder of the World . . . the Mystery Spot!"

"Mystery Spot?" said Elvis. "Where?"

"Look at your legs," said Moo.

All the animals looked. Sure enough, on the downhill side their legs were longer. On the uphill side they were shorter.

"There's something screwy going on here," said Elvis.

"Not in the least," said Moo. "It's simply a matter of science. I'll show you. Everyone turn around and face in the opposite direction."

All the animals turned around. Now

their left legs were longer than their right legs.

"See?" said Minnie. "Science."

"Amazing," said Bea.

Elvis scratched his head.

"Ooohhhhh!" someone moaned.

Moo looked at Minnie. "What?" she said.

"I didn't say anything," said Minnie.

"Ooohhhhh!" moaned the sheep, pointing to the sky.

A pair of long underwear floated above the trees. It turned slowly in the light breeze, and its arms and legs dog-paddled across the sky toward the animals. The sleeves seemed to reach out toward the sheep.

"Wh-What is it?" sputtered a sheep.

"The Sixth Wonder of the World!" said Moo.

The Brood of Shorts

The long underwear rose and dipped on the afternoon breeze.

"Look!" someone shouted. Slowly, from behind the far edge of Wilkerson's Woods, piece after piece of clothing floated through the sky. A blouse was followed by a pair of overalls. A school of socks swam past a brood of shorts. A flock of panty hose flapped above a pajama top that seemed to be searching for a bottom.

"Moops," muttered Moo.

"Moops?" Minnie repeated.

"Moops," said Moo. "This isn't turning out quite the way I had planned."

"What do you mean?" asked Minnie.

"The Sixth Wonder of the World is escaping," said Moo. "Yesterday, after Mrs. Farmer hung out the laundry, I snuck down and borrowed some. I filled up several balloons with helium and stuffed them into the wet clothes. Then I tied one end of some string around each piece of clothing and the other end to a branch of a tree."

"And?" said Minnie.

"And I guess I didn't tie the string tightly enough."

The clothes drifted over a pine tree near the edge of the hill. Two birds began squawking as they floated past.

"Minnie," said Moo, "I think it's time for Madame Minnie to have another vision!"

"Madame Minnie is tired," said Minnie. She picked up the donation jar

THE BROOD OF SHORTS

and looked inside. "We've been at this all day, Moo. And what do we have to show for it? Two dollars and thirty-five cents, an IOU, two eggs, a handful of dried corn, and six metal washers!"

Moo sighed. "We can't give up!"

Minnie put her arm around Moo. She took a deep breath. "Of course not," she said. "Time for another vision! Ooooohhhhhh!" she moaned.

"Madame Minnie is having another vision!" shouted Bea.

The animals surrounded Minnie. The sheep kept their eyes on the flying clothes. "What does it all mean?" they asked.

"It means we have to put another nickel in the jar," said Elvis.

"Ooohhhhhhh!" moaned Madame Minnie. "I feel the power of the Sixth Wonder. I must reach out and let the voice

of Moo speak for Madame Minnie."
Minnie pinched Moo on her bottom.

"Ohh!" cried Moo. "I feel the power!"
She rubbed her behind. "I see . . . I see
clothes."

"No kidding," said Elvis.

"I see farmer clothes," said Moo, "flying on the wings of farmer power."

"The farmer's the boss," said Minnie.

"Who has the power to give?" Moo
shouted.

"The farmer!" cried the sheep.

"And who has the power to take away?"

"The farmer!" shouted the pigs.

"And whose clothes watch us from the sky?"

"The farmer's!" the animals shouted.

"Yes," said Moo solemnly. "It's the Sixth Wonder of the World: ordinary clothes filled with farmer power out for their weekly drying. And why do they fly only on Thursdays, you ask? Because Thursday begins with a 'T' and never falls on a Tuesday!"

"That makes sense," said Bea.

"Doesn't it, though?" said Madge.

Two birds swooped down on the pair of long johns as they drifted past the pine tree. Worried that the long johns would land on their nest, the birds pecked at them with their sharp beaks.

The long underwear exploded and then shot up into the air like a rocket. They loop-de-looped and dived toward the animals.

"Run! Hide! Help!" yelled the sheep. The birds pecked and pecked at the clothes, which whizzed toward the animals. A pair of the farmer's jockey shorts drifted down like a parachute and landed next to Elvis.

Elvis picked up the shorts and put them on. "Ahhh," he said. "I was freezing!"

A Hawaiian shirt landed near Hamlet. He tried it on. "Very nice," said Uncle Snort.

The socks buzzed through the middle of the flock of sheep like a swarm of angry bees, then plunged into the trees near the blouse. Only the panty hose escaped the birds. They fluttered on a high current of wind and flew toward Sweetie's Drive-In.

The birds made one last squawk, then settled back into their nest. The animals all tried to catch their breath as the last of the clothes settled on the high branches of the trees.

"What a disaster," whispered Moo. "How am I ever going to return the farmer's clothes?"

Minnie wasn't listening. She stared at a pair of the farmer's shorts that seemed to be floating about ten feet up in the air. "That's odd," she muttered.

"What?" said Moo.

Minnie pointed at the shorts. "Those shorts look like they're floating in midair."

Moo looked. All the animals looked.

"Minnie," said Moo, "those shorts aren't floating . . . they're hanging. They're hanging from a big hook!"

"That's not a hook," Minnie whispered. "That's a horn! A very big horn!"

Suddenly, there was a loud snort, and the farmer's shorts were flung into the air. A huge gray head poked out from the trees. The head snorted again. Its small black eyes squinted at Minnie and Moo. The animals were as still as petrified wood.

"Are you B-B-Big Hoof?" Moo asked.

"Foop!" said the creature.

The Seventh Wonder

Moo gulped. "Are you Big Hoof?" she asked again.

"I don't think so," said the huge gray-headed creature. It stepped out from the trees. "I don't have hooves, exactly. I have toes." The creature looked down at its feet. "They are rather big, though, aren't they?"

"There's nothing wrong with big," Minnie said quickly.

"That's kind of you to say," said the creature.

"Are you going to eat us?" asked Hamlet.

"Ohhh," gasped the creature. "Why

would I do such a terrible thing? I'm a vegetarian."

"I've seen someone like you before," said Moo. "On television. Remember, Minnie? The farmer was away. We watched the PBS special on India and the animals that live there."

Minnie scratched under her turban.

"Don't you remember?" said Moo. "You ate Mrs. Farmer's lemon cream pie."

"It wasn't a whole pie!" said Minnie.

Moo looked at the creature's thick hide. She admired the big horn on its nose. "You're a rhinoceros," she said.

"Indian rhinoceros," said the creature.

"Then I'm right!" shouted Moo. "You're the missing link between dinosaurs and cows!"

"Am I?" said the rhinoceros.

"We're practically cousins," said Moo.

"Really?" said the creature happily. "Well, foop to you!"

"Foop?" said Minnie.

"Hello," said the rhinoceros. "It's the greeting of our species."

Moo looked at the rhinoceros thoughtfully. "How did you get here?"

"Oh!" said the rhinoceros, looking around. "Promise you won't tell? Please? If they find me, they'll take me back."

"To where?" asked Hamlet.

"To the zoo!" said the rhinoceros.

"The zoo?" said Madge. "How did you get out? Did you smash the gates down?"

"Goodness, no," said the rhinoceros. "I walked out! Somebody left the gate open. I've been hiding in these woods. I like it here. But I feel so—" The rhinoceros began to weep uncontrollably.

"There, there," said Hamlet, patting the huge creature.

"I'm sorry to be so emotional," sniffled the rhino. "It's just that freedom has a price. I'm free but I'm alone."

"Not anymore," said Moo. "What's your name?"

"Irene," said the rhinoceros.

"My name is Minnie," said Minnie. "And this is my best friend, Moo. And this is Madge, and her sister Bea, and . . ."

Minnie continued introducing the animals one by one.

"Now you have new friends!" said Moo.

"Thank you," Irene said with a sigh. "Do you live here?"

"Yes, our farm is over there," said Moo, pointing. "Everything on that other side is the Wilkersons' farm."

Moo explained to Irene about farms and how the animals all lived together. She told her about how each farm had a farmer and how crops were raised and sold for money.

"Money can buy things," said Moo. "We're trying to raise money to save our farm."

"Save it?" said Irene. "Save it from what?"

"Save it from being sold," said Minnie. "Our farmer doesn't have enough money to keep it."

"Oh," said Irene. "I don't know much about those things. You don't need money if you live in a zoo."

"Well, money's not everything," said Moo, "but it's important."

"I know," said Irene. "Yesterday two men were chopping wood close to where I was hiding. Money is all they talked about."

Minnie looked at Moo and then back at Irene. "Was one of the men short, with a gray beard, and grumpy?" Minnie asked.

"Yes," said Irene.

"That sounds like our farmer," said Moo. "But who was the other man?"

"He was tall and skinny," said Irene.

"Mr. Wilkerson," said Minnie.

"He seemed very sad," said Irene.

"Why would Mr. Wilkerson be sad?" said Moo. "If anybody should be sad, it should be our farmer. What did they say?"

"Your farmer," said Irene, "said he doesn't have much money, but he would lend the skinny farmer, Mr. Wilkerson, what he could to help him save his farm. They seemed to be very good friends."

"Wait a minute," said Elvis. He looked at Moo. "You said we were losing *our* farm."

"Moo?" said Minnie. "What exactly did you hear?"

"I . . . I . . . I . . ."

"Moo?"

"I heard Mr. Farmer talking to Mrs. Farmer. I heard him say, 'sell the farm,'" said Moo. "As soon as I heard it, I rushed up the hill and—"

"Made plans to save a farm that doesn't need saving!" cried Minnie.

"I almost put a nickel in that jar," said Elvis. "And I still don't have my gift!"

"This can't possibly get any worse!" said Minnie.

"Are you sure?" said Bea, pointing toward the dirt road.

A green Humvee truck screeched to a halt at the edge of it. Several elderly ladies stepped out and looked around. They wore pith helmets, tan hunting jackets, and jodhpurs. One of them scanned the forest with binoculars and gestured toward the woods.

Irene squinted at the figures moving up the hillside. "My eyesight isn't so good," she said. "What are they doing?"

"They're looking for something," said Madge. "They're poking the brush with long poles with hooks on them."

"Oh, my," said Irene. "I know what they're looking for!"

"What?" asked Moo.

"A rhinoceros!" cried Irene.

The Forest Octopus

The animals stood around Irene in the deep shadows of Wilkerson's Woods. They watched the ladies with the long poles jabbing the bushes as they worked their way up the hill.

"Who are they?" asked Moo.

"They're volunteers from the zoo," said Irene. "The animals at the zoo call them the 'Dotty Docents.' They mean well, but something always seems to go wrong when they try to help. Oh, my. I've got to hide. I don't want to go back! The zoo is so depressing. There's no place to go, and people just stand there staring at you,

hoping you'll fall into the moat or something. On one side are the lions. They're
such snobs. They've never said a word to
me, not even a single 'good morning.' On
the other side are the monkeys, and they
never shut up!" Irene began to sob uncontrollably again.

"There, there," said Hamlet, patting the
rhinoceros gently. "Moo will think of
something."

"Moo?" said Minnie.

Moo nodded thoughtfully. "I have a
plan," she muttered.

"Well?" said Minnie.

"Hide!" said Moo.

Quickly, Irene and most of the sheep
hid behind the largest trees in the forest.
They watched silently.

Minnie touched Moo's arm. "Now
what?" she said.

"Act natural," whispered Moo.

"Act natural?" said Minnie. "That's your plan? Moo, we're cows. I'm wearing a purple bathrobe with gold trim and a turban. You're wearing a tuxedo and a top hat!"

"Pretend everything is normal," said Moo.

Minnie looked at Moo in disbelief. "Normal," she repeated. She looked around the woods. She saw the ladies poking the brush with their poles. She saw a pig wearing a Hawaiian shirt. She saw a molted rooster in a pair of jockey shorts accusing some sheep of hiding a gift. And not too far away she saw a rhinoceros sticking out from behind a tree.

"Normal," Minnie repeated.

"*There!*" shouted the lady with the binoculars. She pointed at Minnie and Moo.

"Uh-oh," said Moo.

"Girls, look who's here," said the lady, still pointing at Minnie and Moo. "It's the Stout sisters, Phyllis and Debbie, from Pocahontas Lodge 452!"

"Yoo-hoo! Debbie! Phyllis! It's me, Dottie Maxwell, and the girls from Pocahontas Lodge 453. We're volunteering today at the county zoo. We're looking for a missing rhinoceros."

The ladies hugged Minnie and Moo.

Dottie pinched Minnie on the bottom. "Putting on a few pounds, are we?" She giggled. "Well, aren't we all, girls?" Everyone giggled. Minnie didn't giggle. She raised one eyebrow and looked at Moo.

Moo shrugged.

Dottie patted Hamlet on the head. "Is this your grandson?" she asked Minnie. "What a clever-looking child. He does look like his grandmother, doesn't he, girls?"

The chickens gathered behind Elvis. "My, oh, my," said Dottie. "Short-necked swans. Very rare. And what are those?"

she asked, pointing at Mort and Snort. "Pygmy hippos?"

Dottie noticed Elvis in the jockey shorts. He was standing next to the donation jar. "Aren't you the sweetest," she said. "Look, girls, a baby buzzard in diapers." She picked up the donation jar. "Whom is Pocahontas Lodge 452 saving this month?" she asked.

Elvis rolled his eyes.

"The Forest Octopus," he muttered.

"Wonderful," Dottie said. "The Forest

Octopus!" She scanned the trees with her binoculars. She looked toward the spot where Irene was hiding. "Oh!" she cried. "Over there! I think I see one!"

Irene ducked down. She tried to make herself small. She held her breath.

"Is the Forest Octopus large and gray, with a big horn on its head?" she asked.

No one said a word.

Irene closed her eyes.

"Yes . . . I think I see one. Girls, get your poles ready."

The ladies from Pocahontas Lodge 453 stood at attention, their hooked poles ready for action.

Minnie looked at Moo desperately. All the animals looked at Moo.

"Up," said Moo.

Dottie looked at Moo. "Pardon?"

"Up," said Moo. "The Forest Octopus

lives up in the tops of the forest's trees, like squirrels."

"Oh," said Dottie. "Silly me. I should have known that!"

Dottie looked through her binoculars at the tops of the trees. "No," she said, "I don't see any up there." She looked back at the spot where she thought she had seen something.

"No. Nothing there, either. No," she said, sadly. "I don't see a one. They must be very rare. I hope you're not too late to save them."

At that moment one of the ladies whispered to Dottie and pointed at her watch.

"Oh, dear, it is getting late," said Dottie. "We have a four o'clock meeting with the Dinner-and-Dance Committee at the country club. We're raising money to save the bipedal gastropod, you know."

The animals nodded and smiled.

Dottie sighed. "Thank you, my friends," she said, then turned to the ladies of Pocahontas Lodge 453. "Girls," she announced, "we've failed to find the wayward rhinoceros. So let us turn our failure into a success by joining with our sisters of Pocahontas Lodge 452 to help save the Forest Octopus!"

The ladies applauded, and Dottie passed the donation jar around. It was quickly stuffed with money. As Dottie handed the jar to Elvis one of the ladies gave her a piece of paper.

"Wonderful," said Dottie, reading the paper. "This brings happy tears to my eyes. Gladys has written a special song for you and Lodge 452," she said. "It's called 'Save the Forest Octopus.'"

Gladys rummaged around in her purse

and took out a pitch pipe. She took a deep breath and blew a long, soft note.

Dottie smiled and nodded at Gladys. Gladys and the girls from Pocahontas Lodge 453 sang her song:

"Save the Forest Octopus
Before it goes extinct.
Save the Forest Octopus
My pen is out of ink.

"It has so many uses,
Here are two or three:
Make a folded purple swan,
And call it 'octogami.'

"Take it with you on a hike,
Take it on safari,
Take a little tartar sauce,
Fry up some calamari.

"Throw it 'round the living room,
It's better than a ball,
Watch it stick to everything . . .
The baby's down the hall.

"Roll it up in bread crumbs,
Mix in a little egg,
Far better than a chicken,
Each diner gets a leg!

"Save the Forest Octopus
Before it goes extinct,
Save the Forest Octopus
My pen is out of ink."

Everyone applauded politely. Then the ladies marched off, climbed into the Humvee, and drove away.

The animals all sighed at the same time. They came out from behind the big trees.

"Minnie," said Moo. "Did you see how much money they put in the donation jar?"

"It's stuffed," said Minnie.

"Where is it?" asked Madge.

Everyone looked around for the donation jar. They found it sitting on Elvis's lap. He was hugging it tightly. "My gift," he sang happily. "At last! And it's all mine. Mine! Mine! Mine!"

"That's going to the Wilkersons," said Moo.

"*Mine!*" Elvis shouted, and ran away. But he was in far too much of a hurry. He tripped over a tree root, which sent the jar rolling across the clearing.

The money spilled into the wind.

"My gift!" squawked Elvis.

The money blew high up in the air and across the meadow. It swirled around and around in the wind. Everyone watched helplessly as it rose higher and higher. Soon the money became tiny pepper spots drifting in the sky.

Then . . . it was gone.

It's a Wonder

Moo sighed. "It's all my fault!" she said. "Minnie, I'm through with thinking. You were right. Cows shouldn't think! It only leads to trouble."

"Your thinking helped me," said Irene.

"And thinking gave us the Seven Wonders," said Hamlet.

Minnie looked over at Elvis. "It wasn't all your fault, Moo," she said. She picked up the donation jar that was sitting at Elvis's feet and counted the money that was left. "Sixteen dollars and eight cents," she announced. "Maybe that will help the Wilkersons and our friends that live on their farm."

"I hope so," said Moo. "I'll take the jar over there and put it where they can find it."

"Let's all go," said Irene.

And so, old and new friends marched off to the Wilkersons' farm. When they reached the Wilkersons' old apple orchard, they stopped.

"There's Mr. Wilkerson," whispered Moo, pointing to the farmer, who was sitting on an old wooden bench in his garden. "Hamlet, sneak down and leave the jar just outside the garden gate."

"Okay," said the little pig. He picked up the donation jar and tiptoed to the garden. He left the jar by the gate and quietly tiptoed back to his friends.

Mr. Wilkerson sat looking at his garden. He thought about all the years that he and Mrs. Wilkerson had tended the garden together. He thought about their grandchildren and their long summer visits. He thought about the sounds of laughter in the summer night.

Mr. Wilkerson scooped up a handful of dirt and let it slide through his fingers. "It's just dirt," he muttered, shaking his head. He scooped up another handful and looked at it carefully. "But . . . it's wonderful dirt."

The farmer tossed the dirt into the garden and stood up and stretched. He noticed a thistle growing near the lettuce. He picked up his hoe and walked over to the edge of the garden. Just as he began hoeing the weed he heard Mrs. Wilkerson open the gate.

"Look!" she cried. "Look what I've found!" She held up the donation jar.

"There's money in there!" Mr. Wilkerson said.

"Sixteen dollars and eight cents," said his wife.

"But where did it come from?" asked Mr. Wilkerson.

"I don't know," said Mrs. Wilkerson. "Maybe someone dropped it off to help us."

"Well, it's a wonder," said Mr. Wilkerson. "But I'm afraid sixteen dollars and eight cents isn't—" Mr. Wilkerson froze. He pointed. "Lettuce!" he wheezed.

Mrs. Wilkerson walked over to her hus-

band. "Sweetheart, are you all right?" she asked.

Mr. Wilkerson knelt down on the ground. "*Lettuce!*" he cried, staring at a large leafy head. A twenty-dollar bill was wedged between the leaves.

"Oh, my!" gasped Mrs. Wilkerson.

"Over there," said her husband, pointing. "There's another one!"

"And another one over there!" cried Mrs. Wilkerson.

The Wilkersons scurried around the garden plucking money from heads of lettuce. They even found a pile of bills blown into the corner of the fence.

"Now, this is farming!" he said happily.

Mr. Wilkerson hoed the money out and

made a neat little money pile at his feet. He picked out a fifty-dollar bill and held it up to the light. "Fifty dollars!" he cried. He held it up to his ear and snapped it a few times. He held it up to his nose and inhaled deeply.

Mrs. Wilkerson looked at her husband and laughed. "Are you going to taste it, too?"

"Just checking to see if it's ripe," said the farmer.

Mrs. Wilkerson joyfully stuffed the money into the collection jar as her husband danced around the garden and out the gate. "This should be enough to save the farm!" he cried. Then he stopped. He looked back at the garden.

"What kind of lettuce is that?" he said.

Mrs. Wilkerson shrugged.

"Whatever kind it is," said the farmer,

"I'm going to plant twice as much next year!"

Minnie and Moo and their friends walked back to their farm under the late-afternoon sun. When they got to the top of the hill, they saw the farmer putting his tools back into his toolbox. He laid his

glasses on the seat of his tractor and car-
ried the box into his workshop.

Moo looked at Irene. She looked at the
tractor again.

"I'll be right back," she called, walking
toward the barn.

The rest of the animals sat down to rest under the old oak tree. Irene reached over and gently touched Minnie on the arm.

"Thank you for being so kind to me," Irene said. "But . . . I should go."

"Go?" said Minnie. "Why?"

"Look at me," said Irene. "I'm a rhinoceros. I escaped from a zoo. People will be looking for me. I might get you in trouble! It's best if I go."

"You don't want to go back to chatty monkeys, snobby lions, and cement floors," said Hamlet.

Irene looked at the cool grass growing at her feet. "No," she said softly. "But—"

"Please," said Madge. "You can stay in the barn with the rest of us."

All of the animals agreed. All except Elvis. Elvis wasn't listening. He was too busy staring at his featherless chest.

"Man, I could use some sunscreen," he muttered. "Is my back red?"

"Elvis!" said Minnie. "Don't you ever think about anyone but yourself? We're talking about Irene."

"Who?" Elvis asked.

At that moment Moo huffed and puffed back up the hill.

"Irene is afraid to stay," said Minnie. "She's afraid that if the farmer sees her, she'll get us all into trouble."

"Well," said Moo. "I was thinking—"

"Again?" said Minnie. "I thought you gave that up."

Moo shrugged. "We are what we are," she said.

"I've heard that before!" said Minnie.

"A friend of mine said it," said Moo.

Minnie smiled and put her arm around Moo. "So . . . ," she said.

"I was thinking," said Moo, "that if we painted Irene black and white, and if we slip her between Bea and Madge in the barn—"

"Moo," said Minnie, "don't you think that tomorrow, when the farmer comes for the early milking, he's going to notice something a little strange? The farmer is going to be able to see the difference between a rhinoceros and a cow."

Moo smiled. "Not without these!" she said, holding up the farmer's glasses.